ROCK'N MY WAY TO ROYALTY

Special thanks to Venetia Davie, Ryan Ferguson, Charnita Belcher, Tanya Mann, Julia Phelps, Sharon Woloszyk, Nicole Corse, Rita Lichtwardt, Carla Alford, Renata Marchand, Michelle Cogan, Julia Pistor, Rainmaker Entertainment and Patricia Atchison and Zeke Norton.

Published in the United States by Random House Children's Books, a division of Penguin Random House LLC, 1745 Broadway, New York, NY 10019, and in Canada by Random House of Canada, a division of Penguin Random House Ltd., Toronto. Random House and the colophon are registered trademarks of Penguin Random House LLC.

ISBN 978-0-553-52435-2 (trade)
ISBN 978-0-553-52436-9 (lib. bdg.)
ISBN 978-0-553-52437-6 (ebook)

randomhousekids.com

Printed in the United States of America
10 9 8 7 6 5 4 3 2 1

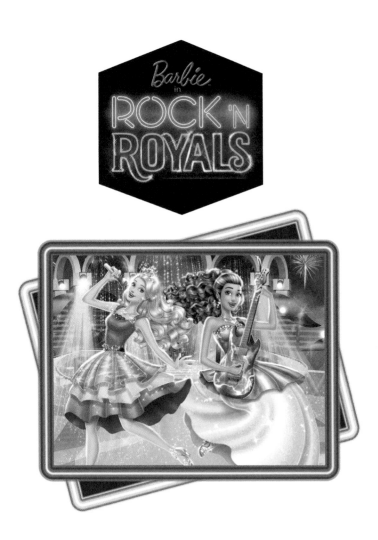

Adapted by Molly McGuire Woods
Based on the original screenplay by Marsha Griffin
Illustrated by Ulkutay Design Group

RANDOM HOUSE 🏠 NEW YORK

In the backseat of a limousine, Princess Courtney fiddled with the magic royal scepter in her lap. She was eager for her two weeks at Camp Royalty to begin! Learning insider princess tips and living on the camp's private island would be amazing. Plus, she would meet other royals her age. Best of all, there would be no official duties—just fun. Courtney couldn't wait!

Behind Princess Courtney, an SUV raced along the same road.

"I was supposed to be there, like, five minutes ago!" Erika complained from the backseat. As a world-famous pop star, Erika was used to traveling. But somehow she was always late.

"I'm not the one who slept through her alarm," the driver joked. "Why did you cancel your tour to go to Camp Pop anyway?"

Erika brushed her blue-streaked hair out of her face. "Being in the spotlight can get kind of lonely," she admitted. "I'm surrounded by people, but no one really feels like a friend."

The driver nodded in understanding.

"Don't get me wrong," Erika continued. "I love performing. But maybe things will be different at camp." Pop stars from all over the world came to Camp Pop to learn about music—rock 'n' roll, country, hip-hop, you name it. They also came to learn cool dance moves. Erika was sure she would fit in. New tunes and new friends—what could be better?

The limo pulled into a parking lot. Princess Courtney nervously smoothed her poufy pink gown. All around her, she saw other princesses in beautiful dresses and glittering crowns. She also saw kids in trendy outfits and big sunglasses. Many carried musical instruments. *Those must be the pop stars,* Courtney thought.

Camp Royalty and Camp Pop were located on the same private island. But the camps were more rivals than friends. The camp directors didn't get along, so rock and

royalty didn't mix anywhere on the island.

Courtney looked beyond the crowd. Two fancy yachts were docked in the water. One would take the royals to Camp Royalty. The other would sail to Camp Pop. Now Courtney had to figure out which line to join!

A man near one yacht called out the names of the royalty. He checked them off a list as they boarded one of the boats. "Princess Aubray of Allanbrooke! Princess Olivia of Bellmere!"

This looks right, Princess Courtney thought as she joined the line.

"Erika of . . ." The man looked at her. "That's odd." He studied his list. "There's

no kingdom listed. Are you Erika?"

Courtney shook her head.

A girl with blue-streaked hair rushed over. She carried a beat-up guitar case. "Here!" Erika shouted. "Sorry I'm late."

Courtney frowned. Erika certainly didn't *look* like a princess. But if her name was on the list, she must be.

Erika hurried on board the royal yacht.

Then it pulled away from the dock.

"Wait!" Princess Courtney shouted. "You forgot me. I'm Courtney!"

But it was no use. The yacht was already gone.

Just then, Princess Courtney heard a voice. "Did you say 'Courtney'?"

A lady with short spiky hair pointed at her.

Princess Courtney nodded.

"Come with me," the woman said. She hurried Courtney onto the other yacht. It was going to Camp Pop.

Uh-oh.

A short boat ride later, Princess Courtney arrived at Camp Pop. The camp director welcomed everyone.

"I'm Finn Oxford," he said. "Who is ready to rock?"

There was no doubt about it: Courtney was in the wrong place. She made her way through the crowd.

"Watch where you're going," a girl with wild punk-rock hair snapped.

"My apologies," Courtney said. "I am a bit . . . lost."

"No kidding," the girl said. "Looks like Cinderella took a wrong turn at the ball."

Courtney felt stung.

"Don't worry about Sloane," said a younger boy. He nodded toward the mean girl.

"Yeah," said a girl who was with him. "She's super talented and super grumpy."

Courtney smiled. "Would you two mind pointing me toward the office?"

The boy and girl showed her the way. At least not everyone at Camp Pop was mean.

In the office, Courtney explained her situation to Finn Oxford and his assistant, Stevie.

"It looks like there's been some type of clerical glitch," Finn said. "But it's kind of late. Stevie will set you up with lodging for one night . . . two at the most!"

Courtney forced a smile. She followed Stevie across camp to a sleek modern building. She heard music pumping. Stevie pointed to a room with a glass door. Two girls were inside, surrounded by musical instruments. "Hello?" Courtney called.

A girl wearing glitzy pink cowboy boots looked up from her guitar. "Come on in!" she

said. "Make yourself at home. I'm Rayna, and this is Zia." She pointed to the girl next to her, who was wearing headphones.

"Pleased to meet you," Courtney said. She could feel her new roommates checking out her gown.

"What's your music style?" Zia asked.

"I don't really have one," Courtney admitted. "I'm a princess."

"Whoa," Zia said. "Am I supposed to bow or something?"

Courtney smiled and shook her head. It was going to be a long night.

On the other yacht, Erika noticed that the passengers all wore fancy gowns. None of them had musical instruments. *Something is wrong here,* she thought.

When they docked, a woman wearing a large pearl necklace welcomed them. "I am Lady Anne, owner of Camp Royalty," she said with a curtsey. "Here you will learn to serve your kingdoms with style and elegance. A magical experience awaits!"

Oh no. Erika slapped her forehead. She was at the wrong camp! She needed to find the office and correct this mistake!

Erika set down her guitar case. A passing princess tripped over it.

"That thing is in my way!" the princess huffed. She looked at Erika's outfit. "What kind of kingdom allows its royalty to dress like *that*?"

"Princess Olivia, hurry up!" someone called. Erika watched the mean girl dash away. And she thought being onstage was lonely.

Erika found the main office. She told Lady Anne and her assistant, Clive, that there had been a mix-up.

Lady Anne said it would have to wait

until tomorrow. "Clive will find you a place to stay tonight."

Clive led Erika to a tree house castle. It looked straight out of a fairy tale! Erika climbed to the balcony and opened the door. Inside, she saw dazzling golden furniture. Velvet drapes hung from the windows. It was a room fit for princesses.

"May I help you?" asked a girl in a long red dress.

Another girl in the room wore a green gown.

"Lady Anne said I could stay here," Erika told them.

Her roommates introduced themselves

as Princess Genevieve and Princess Aubray.

"Are you a pop star?" Princess Genevieve asked. She stared at Erika's blue leggings and sequined shirt.

Erika nodded. Tomorrow couldn't come soon enough.

The next morning, Princess Courtney's roommates were getting ready for their first full day at Camp Pop.

"This year we get to learn about special effects!" Zia exclaimed.

Rayna looked at Courtney. "I'm guessing that's not a princess's kind of thing," she said. "Unless you want to check it out . . ."

Courtney bit her lip. She needed to see how her transfer was going. But special effects sounded fun. Courtney stuffed her scepter into her pocket. Then she raced after the girls.

Over the next couple of days, Princess Courtney had a blast! She rocked out on a microphone and tried country dancing. She even met some other super-nice campers, like hip-hop star Marcus.

A princess had so many rules. But at Camp Pop, everyone wanted to be free and stand out. No one was afraid to try new things. It was such a nice change! Princess Courtney didn't even mind when Finn Oxford explained that her transfer would take a few more days. She wasn't a pop star, but she was having a royally good time pretending she was!

Across the island, Erika watched princesses Aubray and Genevieve get ready for their first day at Camp Royalty.

Genevieve waved her magic royal scepter through the air. A shimmering class schedule appeared before them.

Erika gasped. "How did you do that?" She had seen many special effects onstage, but none as cool as that!

"With my scepter, of course. All royals have one," Genevieve replied. She looked at the schedule. "We have scepter training first. Then tea party etiquette. Then unicorn grooming. I suppose we *could* bring you with us," she said, looking at Erika. "Unless you need to get going?"

Erika frowned. She wanted to go to Camp Pop. But how many chances would she have to see real unicorns? "Wait for me!" she cried.

Over the next couple of days, Erika discovered that being royal wasn't as boring as she thought. She made rainbows with a magic scepter. She brushed a *real* unicorn.

She also played in the royal orchestra. That was *very* different from her solo act. Erika had to admit, being part of the group felt nice. She even daydreamed about how things could be if her transfer to Camp Pop never got approved! Lady Anne said it should only take a couple more days. But Erika was having too much fun to notice!

One afternoon, she had singing class. Erika was excited to finally do something familiar. In the choir room, she listened as the royals sang. She took a deep breath and began to sing, too. Slowly, all the royals around her stopped to listen. Erika's voice was beautiful!

Just then, Lady Anne and her assistant, Clive, passed the choir room. They stopped to listen. Lady Anne liked what she heard.

"I have never heard such a magnificent voice!" Lady Anne whispered to Clive. "Pity it will go to waste at Camp Pop." Then she had an idea. She had often thought about hosting a singing competition between Camp Royalty and Camp Pop. Now, with a real pop star at Camp Royalty, she would have the upper hand. She whispered her plan to Clive.

That afternoon, the leaders of each camp made a surprise announcement. In two days, Camp Pop and Camp Royalty would host their first-ever sing-off competition! Each camp would perform one song. Judges would decide the winner. Rehearsals began first thing in the morning.

What none of the campers knew was that the sing-off was part of Lady Anne's plan to get rid of Camp Pop and expand Camp Royalty. It was no secret that Camp Pop and Camp Royalty always tried to outdo each other. But this time, Lady Anne had raised the stakes. The sing-off winner would own the entire island! The other camp would be forced to close.

Lady Anne planned to use Erika as Camp Royalty's secret weapon. Finn Oxford figured his whole camp of pop stars would put up a good fight. But only one thing was certain: the campers had a lot more to lose than they realized.

The next morning, Princess Courtney's roommates picked out their rehearsal outfits.

"This sing-off is going to be awesome!"

Zia said as she looked through her closet.

"Those royals aren't going to know what hit them!" Rayna cried. She glanced at Courtney. "No offense, Courtney."

Courtney shrugged. "I'm not offended. I've never even been to Camp Royalty. You guys will be amazing."

Zia raised an eyebrow. "Don't you mean we?"

Rayna nodded. "As long as you're here, Princess, you're one of us!"

Courtney smiled. A part of her wished she really belonged at Camp Pop.

"But we should work on your wardrobe," Zia added.

Courtney had a better idea. She whipped out her magic royal scepter. She waved it over her dress. Sparkles flew as her gown changed into a glittery skirt. Her tiara

vanished. A funky bow sat on top of her head instead. She was ready!

Zia and Rayna clapped. "Now, that's an outfit!" Rayna cheered.

"Me next!" Zia cried. The girls giggled.

Meanwhile, Erika's roommates were also preparing for rehearsals.

"You must be psyched about going head-to-head with Camp Pop," Erika said.

"Well . . . not really," Princess Aubray confessed.

"We're good, but not that good," Princess Genevieve admitted.

"You can do this," Erika encouraged

them. "If you need any help while I'm still here, I'll do what I can."

"You would do that for us?" Genevieve asked.

"Of course!" Erika replied. "That's what friends do."

Genevieve and Aubray threw their arms around her. Erika grinned. It felt wonderful to help her friends. Maybe that was why the thought of transferring to Camp Pop now made her sad.

The next day, Finn Oxford found Courtney rehearsing.

"I haven't been able to make any

headway with Camp Royalty about your transfer," he admitted.

Courtney smiled. A few days ago, she would have been upset at that news. But now she felt excited. "It's fine, really," she replied. "I'm having a good time here. Nobody's afraid to stand out or be different or just be silly. It's so much fun. I'd actually love to stay! Is that okay?"

Finn looked shocked. Then he said, "Certainly, Princess."

Courtney was ready to rock!

Across the island at Camp Royalty, Erika was modeling a new gown for her

friends, when Lady Anne entered the room.

"Erika, your transfer to Camp Pop has hit a snag," she said.

"That's okay," Erika replied. "I've made some great friends here."

"Lovely," Lady Anne replied. "You know, I heard you sing yesterday. A talent like yours is a rare find." The director narrowed

her eyes. "I only wish you could remain here and compete in the sing-off as a member of Camp Royalty."

Erika was flattered—and excited. "Wow! Thank you! I could stay."

"Splendid!" Lady Anne exclaimed. Her plan was coming together so easily.

Later that day, Courtney took out some sheet music. She began to sing a new song she had been working on.

As she sang, Marcus, Rayna, and Zia walked in. They couldn't believe their ears. Courtney sounded amazing! Who knew Courtney could sing like that—or write her own music? They picked up their instruments and began to play along with her.

Suddenly, Sloane barged into the room. "What was that?" she asked angrily. "We

have a competition coming up. Maybe you should practice the actual number we're performing." She turned toward Courtney. "Okay with you, Princess? You are out of your league. Maybe you should go back where you belong."

Courtney's eyes filled with tears. Was Sloane right? Was it a mistake to stay?

"I need some fresh air," she said, and raced out the door.

Meanwhile, Erika was practicing with the royals. Princess Olivia, the strongest soprano, led them in the chorus. Erika raised her voice to add more harmony.

"Cut! What was that?" Olivia snapped.
She glared at Erika. "You can solo all you
want at Camp Pop. But at Camp Royalty,
we do things as a group. Perhaps you should

go to Camp *Diva*." She put her hands on her hips.

Erika felt her cheeks turn red. She hadn't meant to outshine the others. Maybe she would never really fit in here . . . or anywhere. She dashed out the door before anyone could see her tears.

Courtney walked along the shore, sadly singing to herself.

"That's beautiful," a voice said.

Startled, Courtney stopped singing. She looked at the girl with blue-streaked hair standing in front of her. "Sorry, I didn't see you there."

"Hey, I know you," Erika said.

Courtney nodded. "We met on the dock."

"Right! When I was trying to make the boat . . . the wrong boat, that is."

"Wait—*you're* the one who's supposed to

be at Camp Pop?" said Courtney.

Erika nodded. "And you're the one who's supposed to be at Camp Royalty!"

The girls laughed.

"We could just switch camps," Erika suggested.

Courtney thought it over. After what Sloane had just said, maybe switching was the right answer. "I don't see why not," she said.

It was settled. Princess Courtney would return to Camp Royalty. Erika would join the other pop stars at Camp Pop. They would both be where they belonged. So why were they still standing there?

Courtney thought about all she had accomplished at Camp Pop. With the help of her friends, she was breaking out of her princess shell. It was fun to just be herself—without all the rules of royalty! How could she leave that feeling of freedom behind?

Erika understood. Her life on tour was always so lonely. She had never felt like she truly belonged anywhere—until her time at Camp Royalty. Giving that up would be so hard!

"You know," Erika suggested, eyeing Courtney, "we could always *not* switch camps. Keep things the way they are . . ."

Courtney was relieved. As bad as things

were, she knew she could count on her friends at Camp Pop to help her through.

"True. There's only a week left," she agreed. "See you at the sing-off, then?"

Erika grinned. She looked as relieved as Courtney felt. The girls hugged goodbye and went to find their friends.

Back at Camp Royalty, Erika apologized for running out. Then she and her friends continued to rehearse.

"Better . . . ," Erika coached. "But the harmonies have got to be tighter."

Olivia crossed her arms. "We don't need a one-hit wonder telling us what to do."

Erika fumed. Why couldn't Olivia see that she was trying to help?

"Fine!" Erika snapped. "You want to go down in flames, be my guest!" She stormed out of the room again.

Erika marched toward the main office. It had been a mistake to come back. She would switch to Camp Pop once and for all. At least they would appreciate her talent.

When she reached the office, she heard Clive talking on the phone.

"I am the smartest," Clive said, dancing around the room. "No one else could have masterminded a plan to make sure Camp Royalty won the sing-off!"

Erika bit her lip. What was Clive talking about? She listened closer, careful to stay hidden.

"I've bribed a judge. In just a few days, Camp Royalty will win. Finn Oxford will have no choice but to close Camp Pop for good!"

Erika clapped her hand over her mouth. The competition was rigged! She had to warn her friends.

Back in their room, Erika told Genevieve and Aubray about Clive's plot. "Even worse,

he and Lady Anne have made some kind of bet with Camp Pop. The loser of the sing-off has to shut down for good!"

Her roommates started to panic.

Erika held up her hands. "I have an idea. But I need your help for it to work. . . ."

That night, Erika and her friends snuck over to Camp Pop. They needed to talk to Princess Courtney.

"What are you doing here?" Courtney asked Erika when they found her.

Erika explained her plan. "The futures of Camp Pop and Camp Royalty are on the line. The only way we can save them is for *everybody* to work together. Do you think you can get the pop stars on board?"

"I'll try," Courtney promised. Rehearsals hadn't exactly been going smoothly for her either. But Courtney knew this wasn't just about her—it was about all of them. Time was running out. With only one more day before the sing-off, she had to try.

Twenty-four hours later, the sun was shining over both camps. It was sing-off day! In a big arena, campers were ready to watch the competition.

"Welcome to the first ever sing-off between Camp Royalty and Camp Pop!" Lady Anne announced.

Finn introduced the judges. It was time to begin.

Courtney and Erika waited backstage with their groups. They had stayed up all night practicing a totally new and totally *secret* sing-off number. It would be amazing!

The plan was for both camps to perform the new number as one big group. That way, the judges wouldn't be able to pick a winner. Both camps would have to stay open!

Courtney and Erika eyed each other nervously. The music swelled. It was now or never.

Performers from Camp Royalty took the stage first. Erika led them in their song. Everything appeared normal. But then, in the middle of their performance, the singers from Camp Pop jumped onstage. Fireworks exploded. The two groups performed a mash-up of their original songs—together! Then they switched to the secret song they had spent all night rehearsing.

Lady Anne and Clive looked shocked. What was happening? Why were the two groups singing *together*?

Onstage, Courtney felt the music in her soul. She caught Erika's eye. Erika winked back. *Now*.

Courtney tossed her microphone high in the air. Lights flashed. The stage filled with swirling smoke and glitter. The fog lifted as Courtney caught her microphone. Her blond hair had changed to bright pink! She

wore a sparkling top and a short tulle skirt instead of her ball gown. Talk about rocker chic!

Erika's outfit was different, too! Her metallic pink-and-blue dress glittered with tiger stripes. The crowd roared.

Erika's and Courtney's friends gathered

around them for the final part. They raised their voices. They sang for their new friendships and for the camps that meant so much to them. They sang for each other and all they had learned. They sang for everyone who had ever felt different.

As they hit their last notes, the crowd went wild! Erika and Courtney grinned at each other. They had done it! But would it work?

Lady Anne crossed her arms. She looked furious. Finn looked confused.

After a few moments, two judges were undecided. The third judge was the one Clive had bribed. She chose Camp Royalty as the winner. Camp Royalty cheered!

But then Lady Anne and Finn interrupted. They decided to overrule the third judge's vote. They declared both camps the winner!

Yes! Erika and Courtney bumped fists. Now both camps would have to stay open!

Near the stage, Lady Anne and Finn Oxford were whispering to each other. What could that mean? Then Lady Anne picked up the microphone.

"Finn and I have worked out our differences," she announced. "We've been blaming each other for some pretty old mistakes, and we pushed you guys to take

sides. But those days are over! Starting next summer, our two camps will merge! We will create one place where we can celebrate rock and royalty alike!"

The audience cheered.

Courtney and Erika high-fived.

"So . . . any plans for next summer?" Courtney asked.

Erika grinned. "Want to room together?"

Courtney nodded and hugged her new friend. Then she looked at the campers in the crowd. Some wore gowns and some wore leather jackets. Some had punk-rock hairstyles and some wore jewels.

But Courtney knew one thing: no matter how different they were, each camper deserved a place where he or she could fit in—or stand out. And a camp that let them do both? That was music to Courtney's ears. She picked up her microphone and nodded at Erika. Then she turned to the crowd.

"Who's ready to rock?"